TIME
for Sale

Written by Val Jones
Illustrated by Kim Roberts
Designed by Peter Shaw

Published by Mimosa Publications Pty Ltd
PO Box 779, Hawthorn 3122, Australia
© 1995 Mimosa Publications Pty Ltd
All rights reserved

Distributed in the United Kingdom by
Kingscourt Publishing Limited
PO Box 1427, London W6 9BR, England

Distributed in Australia by
Rigby Heinemann
(a division of Reed International Books Australia Pty Ltd)
22 Salmon Street, Port Melbourne, Victoria 3207

Distributed in New Zealand by
Shortland Publications Limited
2B Cawley Street, Ellerslie, Auckland

03 02 01 00 99 98
10 9 8 7 6 5 4 3
Printed in Hong Kong through Bookbuilders Ltd

ISBN 0 7327 1562 8

TIME
for Sale

VAL JONES
Illustrated by Kim Roberts

There were only two things Herman wanted out of life – he wanted to be very rich, and he wanted to be rich very quickly. Actually, he never had more than one coin at a time in his patched pocket. He spent his days dreaming of making money without having to work for it.

One day, a stranger arrived in town, pulling an old wooden cart with a shabby leather bag inside it. He sat down to rest in the park. Herman, watching him, began to wonder what was in the bag. Perhaps it was something valuable! He walked over and, without even a word of greeting, demanded to know what the bag contained.

"Something of great value," said the stranger mysteriously, "and yet something that I would gladly give away."

Herman was puzzled. "If it's so valuable, why would you give it away? What is it?"

The stranger looked up at Herman and sighed. "Time," he said. "What is in my bag is time."

"Time!" repeated Herman impatiently. "How can you give away time?"

"Very easily," the stranger replied, "but only if you really want to, and only to someone who really needs it."

"If people need time badly enough, why can't you sell it to them?" asked Herman, who was already hoping that this might be a way of making a lot of money for himself.

"Well," explained the stranger, "I didn't mean that you *can't* sell it, only that you *shouldn't*. If someone gets even one minute too much, it can cause a lot of trouble. Have you ever tried to take back one minute's trouble?"

But by now Herman was too excited to listen. "I don't care about all that!" he shouted. "I want that bag! Sell it to me, I say!"

"I have already told you that I would gladly give it away," said the stranger. "I ask for no money, but here is a warning. If you sell the time, you will have to pull this cart around for the rest of your life. You can only get rid of it by learning to give time away, or by finding someone who wants the bag more than you do at this moment."

Herman was not interested in warnings. He could hardly believe his

luck: something for
nothing; and something he
could sell! Without stopping to
think how the stranger had come by
the bag in the first place, or even to
thank him, Herman grabbed the cart and
ran down the road. "Time for sale," he
muttered to himself. "I'm going to be rich!
I'm going to be rich!"

The stranger watched him go. He straightened his back and smiled, as if a great burden had at last been lifted from him.

Herman hadn't gone very far before he stopped and opened the bag, eager to see what was inside. He carefully undid the worn-out buckle and peeped in. He discovered ... a huge clock! Its face had faded and cracked with age, but it was still working. As he turned it

around he noticed a set of instructions on the back. All he would need to do to make time to sell would be to turn the hands back!

It didn't take long for Herman to find his first customers. As he was passing by the beach, he met a group of fishermen bringing in their haul. Although their nets were already overloaded, they were saying to one another, "If only we had another ten minutes before the tide turns. What a catch we would make!"

Herman put down the cart and scurried across the wet sand toward them. "Do you need some more time? I have some extra time right here in my cart," he told them. "I could sell you ten minutes."

The fishermen stared in disbelief. "How is it possible to buy time?" they asked.

"Easily," said Herman. "But if you don't hurry, it will be too late. The tide will turn and take the fish with it."

At first, the fishermen thought that Herman might be trying to trick them, but they finally decided to put his strange offer to the test. After all, if the magic worked, they could make the biggest catch of the season!

Once Herman had collected the money, he dragged the bag on to the sand and, opening it carefully, revealed the contents. The fishermen stared at Herman's ancient clock – a clock older than any they had ever seen before.

"Prepare yourselves!" he commanded, secretly wondering what would happen. As soon as the nets were ready, he slowly began to turn back the hands of the magic clock. One minute ... two minutes ...

three minutes … They all listened as the hands creaked back through time. Everything went still, until there was a silence deeper than the sea itself.

And then, instead of the washing of the waves on the sand, all that could be heard was a hollow ticking as the bought time began to pass. Before the ticking stopped, the nets had been filled once more. The happy fishermen sang as they prepared their fish for market.

Herman was delighted that his patched pocket now bulged with money. He had begun to pull his cart away when he heard one of the fishermen call after him: "Bring your clock to us at the same time tomorrow. We will pay you double if you double the time!"

Herman remembered the stranger's warning, but said to himself, "Surely helping the fishermen can't cause any trouble."

The next afternoon, Herman returned to the beach. This time he wound the hands of the clock back twenty minutes. Once more, the fishermen sang as they brought in their mighty catch. Once more, just as Herman was pulling his cart away, they called after him: "Come back tomorrow. We will triple your first payment if you triple the time."

On the third night, the fishermen paid Herman their money and began their extra thirty minutes of fishing. But they had hardly started to haul in their nets when they found themselves being buffeted about by the waves.

Suddenly the ocean seethed with enormous fish. "Fools! Greedy fools!" they cried. "Weren't your hauls big enough

before? You didn't stop to think of us! If
you catch all the smaller fish, there will be
nothing left for us to eat! Do you think
you can keep taking more and more?"

The fishermen were stunned and terrified. They didn't know what to do. "Please forgive us," they begged, trembling with the fear of being drowned. "We didn't mean any harm to you; we thought only of ourselves. Let us go safely! We promise never again to take more than our share of fish from the ocean."

At that, slowly, the waters became calm once again. "Very well," said the fish, "but the ocean does not welcome that stranger, nor the magic which is born of greed. You must drive that greedy villain and his clock away!"

The frightened fishermen vowed to do as they were told. But Herman had already taken up his cart and crept away.

He had seen what was happening, and wanted to be gone before the fishermen had a chance to demand their money back. He cared little for them and even less for the fish. "There are plenty of places where I can seek my fortune," he thought. And with both pockets now full of money, he set off for the countryside.

The next day, he came to a large forest. He followed a pathway through the trees until he came to a

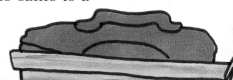

clearing, where he was glad to sit down and rest. Taking out a handkerchief, he wiped his face. "It's hard work pulling this cart," he said to himself. "That bag seems to get heavier the further I go!"

As he rested, Herman became aware of voices nearby. He stood up and dragged his heavy cart further along the path. He soon came to a group of woodcutters, busily cutting down tall trees and sawing them into logs.

As they worked, they talked among themselves. "I wish we had time to cut more logs before nightfall," one said. "Then we could sell more."

"Yes, but it's already starting to get dark – and we can hardly stop the sun setting," laughed another.

Herman listened with increasing interest, and wondered what would happen if he dared use the clock again. Then the thought of more money overcame any caution that he might have felt. "If you need more time, I could sell you an hour," he said.

"What do you mean?" asked the woodcutters, gathering around him. He pointed to his cart and said, "I have time to sell right here in my bag – if you can afford it."

At first the woodcutters were as wary as the fishermen had been, but soon they agreed. Herman made sure he had collected their money,

and then pulled the clock from his bag. As he turned the hands back one hour, the forest became still and silent. To everyone's amazement, the fading light became strong again, and sunbeams slanted down through the tall trees. The woodcutters sang as they worked and the great trees fell crashing to the ground.

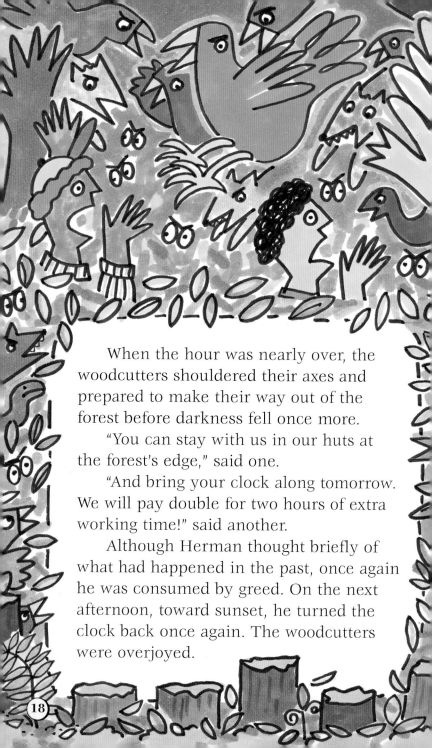

When the hour was nearly over, the woodcutters shouldered their axes and prepared to make their way out of the forest before darkness fell once more.

"You can stay with us in our huts at the forest's edge," said one.

"And bring your clock along tomorrow. We will pay double for two hours of extra working time!" said another.

Although Herman thought briefly of what had happened in the past, once again he was consumed by greed. On the next afternoon, toward sunset, he turned the clock back once again. The woodcutters were overjoyed.

As they loaded the logs, they said, "With an extra *three* hours, we would have even more logs to sell."

And Herman agreed to come back with them again. But the woodcutters had hardly begun to chop at the trees when there was a rustling in the leaves and a scurrying in the grass. Suddenly, huge flocks of birds appeared, screeching angrily and diving at the woodcutters; and from the bushes appeared all kinds of forest animals, biting and clawing.

"Fools! Greedy fools!" they squawked and snarled. "Can't you see what you're doing to the forest? Where will we live if you cut down all the trees?"

The woodcutters were terrified. "Please forgive us," they pleaded. "In our hurry we didn't think of your needs, only of ourselves! Let us go safely! We promise never again to take more than our share of logs from the forest."

"Very well," said the birds and animals, "but in future you must take more care – and you must drive that greedy villain and his clock away!"

The frightened woodcutters vowed to do as they were ordered. But Herman had seen what was happening, and had crept quietly away before they could demand their money back. He cared little for the woodcutters, and even less for the birds and animals of the forest.

Although he would not venture into that part of the country again, there were plenty of places where he could seek his fortune.

Herman set off again, dragging his cart, which seemed to be more of a burden the further he went. Finally, he came to a city. "This bustling city must be full of people who need more time. I will certainly get rich here," he thought. "Then I will live in luxury, in a beautiful house surrounded by a magnificent garden!"

With the money he already had, he was well on the way to fulfilling his dream.

Each day, he trudged down the busy streets selling time. He had no shortage of buyers – everyone was delighted to have extra time because they were able to use it to make more and more money. While they were working harder and getting richer, no one, least of all Herman, noticed that the chimneys were billowing out bigger and bigger clouds of black smoke.

Before long, Herman was so rich that he was able to afford the wonderful house and gardens that he had dreamed of. He became so busy enjoying his riches that he forgot about the angry fishes, birds and animals, and even about the stranger's warning.

Life was very good for Herman, until one spring when something very strange happened. He waited as he usually did at the end of winter for the first buds and leaves to appear in his beautiful garden. But this time he waited and waited in vain. Instead of his garden filling with flowers and leaves, the trees remained bare and stark, and not one green shoot appeared.

The rest of the city was bleak, too – there were no flowers or leaves anywhere! The sun could not break through the thick clouds of black soot and smoke which had been steadily pouring out of the factories and workshops since Herman's arrival in the city.

The people were so troubled by this that they decided to hold a meeting in the park. All the factories and workshops were closed. There was to be no work until they discovered what was wrong. But no one could find any reason why their once bright and happy city should have become so dull and drab. They continued to meet in the park each day, but still they could not explain what had happened.

Then, one day when they arrived there, they noticed some tiny green shoots pushing their way through the soil. Fresh young leaves were beginning to appear on the trees. The factories were closed ... no one was working ... and everything was beginning to grow again. What had happened? Suddenly, they realized what was wrong with their city! Spring would only come when the air was fresh and clean!

"We have choked our city with soot from the factories and workshops ... and all because we have become greedy!" they cried. They were so pleased to see that they had not killed the plants and trees, and so happy to see the sun and the blue sky, that they decided never again to let their greed endanger the city. Then they remembered that it was Herman who had started all this trouble by selling them time.

"He must leave our city!" they shouted, setting off in the direction of his house. Herman saw them coming and heard their angry cries and threats. He tried to leave his house but found himself fixed to the spot. He looked around in desperation, and his gaze fell upon the cart with the leather bag. Then he understood – he simply could not move without the bag of time! Grabbing the cart, he slipped out of the back gate of his magnificent estate with only moments to spare.

He staggered toward the edge of the city, dragging the cart behind him. He had no idea where he would go – for now he was not welcome anywhere.

The cart was beginning to grow so heavy that Herman could hardly pull it. He stumbled on and on until he was exhausted and had to sit down by the side of the road. He did not know how far he had come or where he was.

Suddenly the words of the stranger returned to him. He remembered the

warning that neither the time nor the trouble it caused could be put back into the bag. He recalled what the stranger had said about becoming too greedy. He would have to pull the cart around with him for the rest of his life! His only hope was to find someone who wanted its burden as much as he had when he first demanded it from the stranger. But would there be anyone left who hadn't heard of the damage he had done when he sold time?

Then other words rang in his ears: "It is better to give away time, rather than sell it … but only to someone who really needs it."

"Who could really have need of it?" wondered Herman. Just then, he heard someone calling for help.

He left the cart by the side of the road and followed the cry. For the first time in his life he was running to help someone without thinking of any payment. He found a woman who lay injured and helpless in a ditch. "Please help me," she cried. "My wagon has overturned and I have hurt my leg. If I don't get my goods to market before noon, I will have no money to buy food for my children."

Herman carried her to a comfortable spot and started to load the fruit back on to the wagon. "Tell me how to get to the market," he said; and before long he had taken the wagon to the market, sold the fruit, and returned to the woman with the empty wagon and the money. Herman, without knowing why, felt happier and more satisfied than he had ever felt before.

"How much do I owe you?" asked the woman.

"Nothing," replied Herman.

"Not even for your time?" she asked.

"No," said Herman, smiling, as he realized that he had just discovered how to give away time. From now on, he was always going to give – even if it meant that he had to become poor again himself.

He turned to take up his burden – but the cart and the leather bag containing the ancient clock had disappeared. Herman felt wonderfully free.

The rest of his life was spent helping people by giving away time, just as he had helped the woman. His happiness grew, and so did his love for the birds, the animals, the fish, and the trees. He turned his attention to protecting them, rather than trying to make money.

Herman was forgiven by those he had once hurt, and although he became poor again, he had everything he wanted. He found friendship and happiness: by the sea, in the forests of the countryside, and in the busy cities throughout the land.

TITLES IN THE SERIES